This story is dedicated to
all my grandchildren past,
present, and future.

www.mascotbooks.com

For more information, please contact:
Mascot Books
620 Herndon Parkway, Suite 320
Herndon, VA 20170
info@mascotbooks.com
Second Printing. This Mascot Books edition printed in 2018.

Library of Congress Control Number: 2018902091

CPSIA Code: PRT1018B
ISBN-13: 978-1-68401-706-5

Printed in the United States

Willy Willy Wonkey, You Silly Silly Donkey

Written by
PAMELA LYNCH

Illustrated by
OMAR HECHTENKOPF

Willy Willy Wonkey,

You Silly Silly
Donkey

Willy Willy
Wonkey,
You
Silly Silly
Donkey...

Willy Willy
Wonkey,
You
Silly Silly
Donkey...

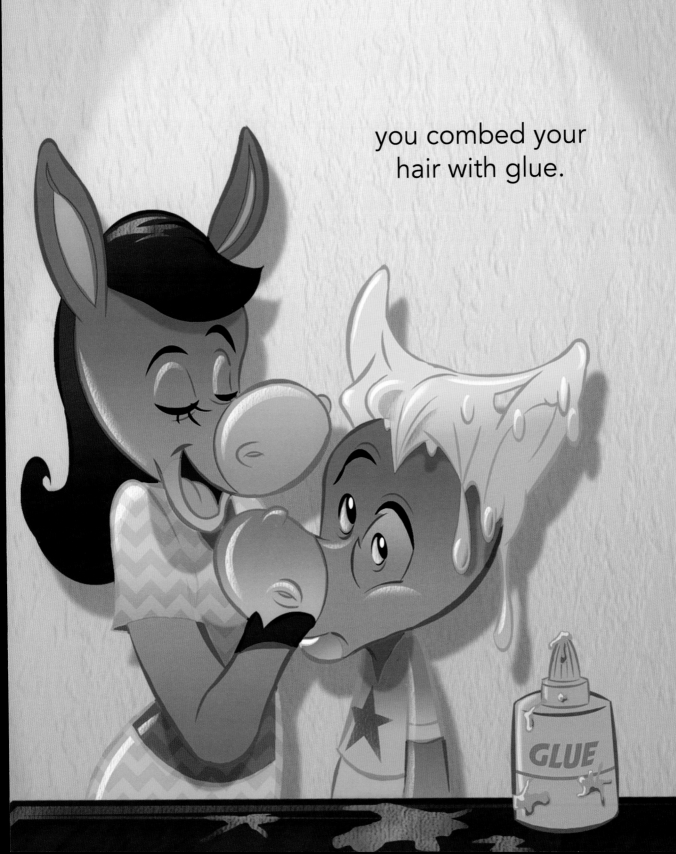

Willy Willy

Wonkey,

You

Silly Silly

Donkey...

your underwear
is on your head.

Willy Willy
Wonkey,
You
Silly Silly
Donkey...

your shirt's inside out.

Willy Willy Wonkey, You Silly Silly Donkey...

your pants are
on backwards.

Willy Willy
Wonkey,
You
Silly Silly
Donkey...

Willy Willy
Wonkey,
You
Silly Silly
Donkey...

your gloves are
on your feet.

Willy Willy Wonkey, You Silly Silly Donkey...

your shoes are
on your hands.

It's okay **Willy Willy Wonkey**, you are a young **silly silly donkey**, you will get things right.

But for now, go
back to bed, it's the
middle of the night.

Love ya,
my sweet
donkey.